The Adventures of Lola Larissa Lily

a little lady bug
finds a fantastic friend

by Lauren Coffey

The Adventures of Lola Larissa Lily,

a Little Bug Finds a Fantastic Friend © 2017

Written by Lauren Coffey

Illustrated by Charles Berton

A Squish Tale Book

For questions or comments, please email the author at Squishtales@gmail.com

Please visit the illustrator at CharlesBerton.com

To Collin, Neela and Aniya

It was a beautiful morning. The sun was just peeking out and kissing the top of the tree line across from Lola Larissa Lilly's home. Lola Larissa Lilly's home was super cool. It had lots of windows, forty seven floors and it was built in 1912.   In 1912, *all* the cool ladybugs had hide outs and all of Lola Larissa Lily's 47 floors had hideouts.

As Lola Larissa Lily woke up and got herself ready, she thought to herself what wonderful adventure would she have today, on *this* day, *today*. She thought and she thought...*hmmm*...I wonder.

As Lola Larissa Lily ate her breakfast of aphids, she wondered what her friends were going to do on this fantastically fabulous day? Lola Larissa Lily wondered where were her friends...wondered...could they play with her?

After chores and breakfast, Lola Larissa Lily headed out to find her friends. Where should she look first?

"Ooooh! I know," thought Lola Larissa Lily, "I'm going to go to the pond!" Lola Larissa Lily twirly twirled and loopdy looped all the way there, excited about what her friends may be doing and what they could do together *today* on *this* day!

Fluttering her wings in excitement, Lola Larissa Lily approached the pond. She could make out faint images of what she was sure were her friends. As Lola Larissa Lily got closer, she saw Fiona Florence Fatima, Fenwick Franklin Fordasque, and Tersey Tabias Terrapine together in the pond.

She shouted loudly, "Hey there! *Hellooooooo everyone!*"

"Hey, Lola Larissa Lily!" said Fiona Florence Fatima as she darted up into the air, flipped and turned her body so that it was like a torpedo, and then dove back into the water.

"Umm…uh…er…ahhhh, guys, does she realize she dove into the shallow end?"

*"Mmmpth…phblt…bblllpt…*I do now!" Fiona Florence Fatima says as she comes up shaking off the muck and the mud, splattering a little on Tersey Tabias Terrapine and Fenwich Franklin Ford a squeeze. Lola Larissa Lily darts and dodges the splatters.

"What's shakin', bacon?" Fiona Florence Fatima asks.

"You, obviously!" Lola Larissa Lily says laughing as she dodges yet another splash of muck flying through the air. "Alrighty, aside from mudslinging, what are you guys up to?"

"We were trying to play water polo but we didn't have enough people," Tersey Tabias Terrapine said. "Yeah, we tried but it turned into monkey in the middle."

Fenwick Franklin Fordasque said, "Yeah, and *I* was in the middle, just because I can hop! How unfair is *that?*"

Lola Larissa Lily laughed and said, "I wish I could have seen that!"

"No, no, no, *no!*" Fenwick Franklin Fordasque exclaimed! There was that one creature that wanted to play and *you*, Tersey Tabias Terrapine, said *no!*"

Tersey Tabias Terrapine said, "Yeah, a creature like no other! It hovered above the water but had no wings!"

"No Wings? But hovered?! How did that happen? Magic?" gestured Lola Larissa Lily.

"I think so!" said Fiona Florence Fatima.

"Maybe it's hocus pocus magic?" said Fenwick Franklin Fordasque.

"No creature without wings can hover! How long have you been in the sun?" Lola Larissa Lily asked. "Did you drink enough water? 'Cause you sound silly and a bit cray-cray!" Lola Larissa Lily laughed.

Fenwick Franklin Fordasque said, "It's easy for me to take care of. *Ribbet, ribbet...*" As his boomerang tongue flies out, he grabs a fly, flicking it back into his mouth.

Tersey Tabias Terrapine said, "Whoa *Where...when... what??* This ain't no fly."

Fenwick Franklin Fordasque said, "This creature was not like any other."

"Okay, okay, let's get off the 'creature' and let's play. What can we play that I can play too?" Lola Larissa Lily asked.

"Um...*hello?* Join us in water polo," they all said in unison.

Lola Larissa Lily said, "Um...*hello?* I can't get wet. Remember my delicate wings? It's why I am covered in a hard shell."

"Okay, okay," said Tersey Tabias Terrapine, "what can we *all* play?"

"I don't know," said Fiona Florance Fatima, "but I know who would..."

Fenwick Franklin Fordasque asks, "Who?"

Meanwhile, back at the ranch…er…meadow, the other larger animals, Laramus Leonard Layton, Zane Zekial Zack, Georgia Gabriella Ginger and Eliza Erma Eloqueesha were playing soccer. Boys verses girls…the girls were winning. The girls usually did, but that was because Eliza Erma Eloqueesha was so much taller than the net.

But…they kept having one tiny problem. They were losing balls in logs, holes, caves and tunnels that were too teeny-tiny for these big animals to get to.

Laramus Leonard Layton tried and tried to get the balls, even with his tail! Eliza Erma Eloqueesha used her trunk with no luck. Georgia Gabriella Ginger tried to use her long, long, long neck but couldn't get her head in past her horns, and she was forlorn. Zane Zekial Zack tried using his legs - they fit but couldn't reach. They tried everything …not happening…nothing worked.

Now with only one ball left they were all trying to decide who got the ball first, when suddenly this creature floated down and hovered in the sky.

"Hi everyone, I can help if you -"

When all of the animals saw this thing, they *jumped* in the air, hair standing on end! They all ran away from this teeny-tiny…magic…creature?

"But wait! Where are you going? I just want to…play… and help."

But it was too late, they all scurried off in different directions. Laramus Leonard Layton even hid in a tree! They all scurried away so quickly that they didn't even hear Sophia Saraphina Serena the delightfully sophisticated... *spider*. It was at this moment Sophia Saraphina Serena the spider felt the saddest she had ever felt before, and she dropped from her web down to rest on a flower, head in her legs, convinced she would *never* have any friends...ever.

At the same time Lola Larissa Lily, who had found DeeDee Delilah Danda on her way to look for Laramus Leonard Layton and the others, was zipping around twirly-twirls and loopdy-loops all over with her *bestest best* friend DeeDee Delilah Danda. They were having so much fun and flying so fast that they didn't see what was coming up in front of them in between the tree branches. But Sophia Saraphina Serena did and yelled out, "No! *Look out!*" Lola Larissa Lily and DeeDee Delilah Danda looked up just in time, swerved and just missed a *huge* spider web!

"Whoaza! Thanks! Who are you?" Lola Larissa Lily asked this odd looking, eight legged creature.

"I'm Sophia Saraphina Serena. I live nearby. I'm finally old enough to go out and explore." Sophia Saraphina Serena hung her head as she said, "I tried several times today," her eyes getting watery with tears, "to make some friends… *sigh,* but with no luck."

Lola Larissa Lily and DeeDee Delilah Danda looked at each other, feeling bad for Sophia Saraphina Serena. "Don't be sad. Don't cry. We can be your friends," DeeDee Delilah Danda said as Lola Larissa Lily nodded in agreement.

"Yes!" Lola Larissa Lily said. "But what do you mean you tried?"

"Oh, that would make me so happy!" exclaimed Sophia Saraphina Serena. She explained to Lola Larissa Lily and DeeDee Delilah Danda how she had tried to help the animals today by offering to make a web as a net for the ball game they were playing in the water, and to help by making webs to stop the balls from getting lost in holes, logs and crevices.

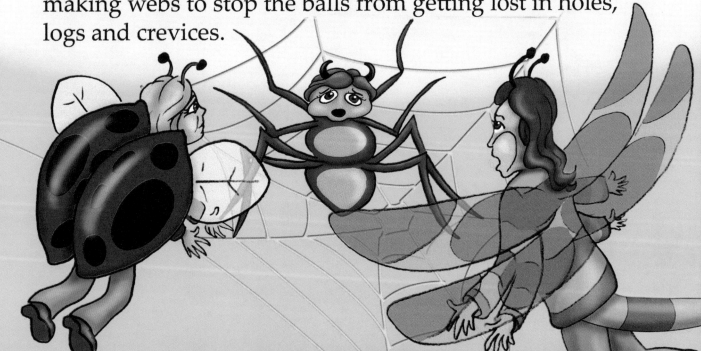

Just as Sophia Saraphina Serena were finishing up explaining why she was sad and how she tried, Fenwick Franklin Fordasque, Tersey Tabias Terrapine, and Fiona Florance Fatima were finally catching up to them from the pond.

"It's the creature!" Fenwick Franklin Fordasque shouted. "Get it!" As he positioned to use his bug-catching boomerang tongue, Tersey Tabias Terrapine and Fiona Florence Fatima jumped into position to help. Things were looking pretty grim for Sophia Saraphina Serena at this moment but Lola Larissa Lily and DeeDee Delilah Danda fluttered to her defense in the nick of time.

"Oh no you don't! She saved us! This is Sophia Saraphina Serena. She is sweet and kind and she is a…er… uh…" Lola Larissa Lily, putting her hand up to her face, whispered, "what kind of insect are you anyway?"

Sophia Saraphina Serena whispered back, "I'm a spider. See my eight legs?"

"Oh!" Lola Larissa Lily whispered back. "I've never met a spider before. I didn't know." Turning back toward Fenwick Franklin Fordasque, Tersey Tabias Terrapine, and Fiona Florence Fatima, she proclaimed, "Spider. Sophia Saraphina is a spider!" Lola Larissa Lily smiles. "A sweet kind spider who just wants to make some friends and play with us. She tried to help you at the pond by making a web she makes from..."

As Lola Larissa Lily was explaining, Laramus Leonard Layton, Zane Zekial Zack, Georga Gabriella Ginger, and Eliza Erma Eloqueesha started to slowly come toward them.

"Yeah," DeeDee Delilah Danda said as the others were back, "then you guys kept losing balls in logs and caves. She was trying to win you over by closing them with her web to stop the balls from getting stuck."

Sophia Saraphina Serena balloon-dropped down from a tree on a spindle of her glistening silk gossamer. "I've been watching you all have fun together for months, but my mommy said I wasn't allowed out yet, and I just thought one of my nets could help for your water polo, Mr. Fenwick Franklin Fordasque and Mr. Laramus Leonard Layton, but you - I'm sorry - lose so many balls, *sooo*, so many," she said, giggling. "I thought blocking might help you. I meant no harm and didn't want to scare you. I float like this from my spider silk. It's so fine sometimes that you can't even see it. It is actually really, really fun! I'm not very big but the web I build is *super strong!*"

Laramus Leonard Layton said with a sheepish smirk "Your webs can really stop one of Eliza Erma Eloqueesha's kicks?"

"Absolutely-wootly!" Sophia Saraphina Serena said.

"Okay, Sophia Saraphina Serena, let's see," Zane Zekial Zack said with a tone of disbelief in his voice.

"Okay…" Sophia Saraphina Serena replied, slightly rattled.

Lola Larissa Lily and DeeDee Delilah Danda flew in close and whispered. "Are you okay? Are you sure about this?"

Sophia Saraphina Serena replied, "I can do this. My web can be as strong as Kevlar in the right thickness. *Hmmm…* I might need a minute though, ladies. Can you have my back?"

"For sure!" Lola Larissa Lily and DeeDee Delilah Danda replied in unison. They looked at each other and winked because they knew what to do. Just because Sophia Saraphina Serena is different, she shouldn't be treated differently. They definitely had her back. They were just getting to know her, but the more they did, the more they liked her. She was so sweet.

"So, Laramus Leonard Layton and Zane Zekial Zack, Eliza Erma Eloqueesha and Georgia Gabriella Ginger were winning again? I thought you said you two were the best players around?"

"Ummm…well actually, we were about to tie but our ball got stuck in a log," Laramus Leonard Layton said, crossing his arms, chest puffed out.

"Let us try to get it out," Fenwick Franklin Fordasque said.

And Tersey Tabias Terrapine and Fiona Florence Fatima both said, "Yes!" at the same time and "Jinx!" at the same time. "No backsies! Hey!" they said, laughing.

"Okay, okay, you two," Lola Larissa Lily said, thinking the plan was working.

All three tried to get the ball out. But it wasn't until they worked together that they were able to get it out of the log.

Fenwick Franklin Fordasque kicked one out of a cave.

Fiona Florence Fatima got another out of a tree and questioned, "The tree? The *tree?* Up here…*really?* Who did this shot? *Sheesh!*"

All the while, Sophia Saraphina Serena was busy working away, blocking up the holes with her web and making a big net between two trees. "I've seen others play this and I think we can all play this together. It's called volley ball," Sophia Saraphina Serena explained. "But first the strength test. Eliza Erma Eloqueesha, are you ready?"

"Yes!" Eliza Erma Eloqueesha replied. "Are *you* ready?" Laughing, thinking there was no way she wasn't going to kick right through the web net.

"I'm so ready and positive this will work. I'll hang out behind the web and won't get hurt."

"But there is a rock wall behind that web net! Are you crazy?" Laramus Leonard Layton exclaimed in a high pitched voice. "I don't want you to get hurt. I like you. Besides, we are friends now!" He smiled and patted Sophia Saraphina Serena on her tiny head with his big paw.

She was beaming with happiness. "Friends," Sophia Saraphina Serena thought. "I finally…have…friends!"

"It will be okay, Laramus Leonard Layton. Trust me. I just found you guys and I'm not losing my new friends now!" Sophia Saraphina Serena giggled as she got into position on the back of the net.

Georgia Gabriella Ginger tapped the ball towards Eliza Erma Eloqueesha with her long, long, long giraffe leg. "Go ahead Eliza Erma Eloqueesha!"

Eliza Erma Eloqueesha got into position to kick the soccer ball through the net. "Okay, ready…set…go!" And Eliza Erma Eloqueesha kicked the ball as hard as she could. She was starting to believe Sophia Saraphina Serena. She thought to herself, "No one is *that* crazy, right?"

Laramus Leonard Layton couldn't take it. "No, little buddy, *nooo!!!* I'll save you!" he yelped. And he leaped with his cat like skills toward the net to block the ball and protect Sophia Saraphina Serena. But he was too late. He just missed the ball.

Laying face down in the grass with paws over his head which was shaking back and forth, Laramus Leonard Layton cried, "No, no, no, no, no, no, my new little buddy! Oh, the horror. The *horror!* The horror. I can't look. I just can't look. It's so sad. So, so sad. So young, so sweet, so nice, so pretty - I can't look." He continued on with the whimpering over what he thought was his newly made, newly smushed friend.

What he didn't realize was that Sophia Saraphina Serena was alright! Her net was so strong, it didn't even budge when the ball hit it!

Sophia Saraphina Serena looked at the others confused. They just looked at her and shrugged their shoulders. Sophia Saraphina Serena's balloon floated through the air over to him and landed on his nose, which was almost as wet as a swamp from his tears.

"Um…what do you say we play some volley ball now?" Sophia Saraphina Serena laughed.

Laramus Leonard Layton muttered, "Oh great, now I'm hearing her voices. I'm going to miss her so much."

"Laramus Leonard Layton it's me, Sophia Saraphina Serena," she said gently, stroking his wet fur with one of her legs. "I'm glad you care. I think we can be…what do you call it? Oh right, best friends!"

"Guy's, you better call the doctor. I swear I can feel her touch me as I hear her voice!" said Laramus Leonard Layton.

In unison the friends said, "Open your eyes! That's because it is Sophia Saraphina Serena! Holy moly, get it together and open your eyes." They all laughed.

"Huh..?" Laramus Leonard Layton said as he slowly opened up one of his eyes while covering the other. He saw a blurry image that slowly came into focus as he opened his other eye. "Sophia Saraphina Serena! Wait. But what, how…huh? Did…you - shouldn't you be smushed?"

Lola Larissa Lily said, "No, her web was as strong as she said, and it didn't even move! It was so cool!"

"Oh, thank goodness!" Laramus Leonard Layton said, jumping up on his feet, feeling slightly silly but very relieved. *"Heh, heh, heh!* Okay, so tell me about this volley ball game we can play." They all listened as Sophia Saraphina Serena explained how to play.

They all played together and everyone realized they were really going to like Sophia Saraphina Serena even though she was so different. I mean she had eight legs instead of six, and could climb, crawl and fly through the air, and make silk from her own body, but guess what? The things that made her different helped make her a very good teammate. Plus, with the help of her webs, they lost a lot fewer balls.

By the end of the day, all of the longtime friends realized they had made a *new* really, *really* good friend! They also realized that today, *this* day, today they almost missed out on the friendship of a *very, very, very* great creature just because she was different.

THE
END

About the Author

A Long Island local from Center Moriches, I began writing stories in 2009 and decided to share them with everyone. I love writing stories that are whimsical in nature that will make children laugh, smile and also point to a moral lesson.

While recovering from a tragic accident that had me out of commission for many months, I focused my energy in a creative direction and drew inspiration from my brother's new Child. This prompted the writing of my first story *"The Adventures of Lola Larissa Lily, a Little Ladybug"* and fueled my writing journey.

Please check out:

Available on Amazon.com and Kindle

Made in the USA
Charleston, SC
24 February 2017